A BWWM
Romance

ALMOST YOURS

Dylan Roxi

ardent artist books
publishing since 2008

Almost Yours

Copyright © 2022-2024 by Dylan Roxi

All rights reserved.

Book Cover and formatting provided by Trisha Fuentes

https://bit.ly/m/trishafuentes

No part of this book may be reproduced in any form or by any electronic or mechanical means, including information storage and retrieval systems, without written permission from the author, except for the use of brief quotations in a book review.

about ardent artist books

➥ **ABOUT US**

Ardent Artist Books was established in 2008

We publish modern and historical romances once a
month!

Get Your FREE List: Published & Upcoming Books
visit our website at:
https://bit.ly/3Wva4o0

➥ **WE HAVE BOOK TRAILERS**

Follow us on YouTube!
https://bit.ly/3W3xn7a

Like, Subscribe & Comment

~

 ## **WE HAVE SERIALIZED FICTION!**

Visit our website today to download one of our stories that unfold in bite-sized pieces!

Each installment is just 99¢!
Paperback $9.99

https://bit.ly/3LsDpJL

~

 ## **LET'S CONNECT!**

Fuel your love of fiction with exclusive content and captivating insights from Ardent Artist Books. Whether you crave the thrill of modern narratives or the timeless elegance of historical fiction, our newsletter delivers a curated selection straight to your inbox. Plus, as a welcome gift, receive a FREE downloadable eBook:

"The Family Fix"

https://bit.ly/49BR3UB

contents

almost yours

one

"YOUR HONOR—"

"Ms. Bailey, I said, that's enough," the judge's lips stretched into a thin, angry line, and her wrinkles sagged like a bulldog's would, "I've heard what I needed to, I've seen what I needed to, and my judgement is to the defendant."

As the gravel bangs against the cool wooden surface, I realize that I had won. My client's family erupted in chairs from the sidelines, and I clicked my pen in satisfaction, eyeing my boss Max who lifted his clapping hands to me.

My opponent quickly gathered her things, her lips tapping with every displeased mumble.

My heart, which was beating out of my chest the entire time, calmed with cold sweat.

I did it.

"Cheers to the woman of the night," Max raises his champagne glass, a big grin on his face as he held me to his side. I couldn't stop the fit of giggles that escaped my lips, or the huge display of my teeth. I was excited. I've won cases before, but they were minor. This one was huge.

I saved a man from life in prison, you had no idea the weight that was on my shoulder almost every night, or how many times my fiancée Leo had to warn me that I'll drive myself crazy.

Tonight, I could relax. I could take a deep breath, and feel proud of myself without that dull ache that often remained in my stomach.

"You did great, *Sandy*-Shandy," Max's chuckles were deep.

Sandy-Shandy. A cute office nickname for those who adored me in the office.

"Thanks, Max. Enjoy your drinks, allow me to make a quick phone call."

"Of course."

As I stepped away from his grip, I smiled through the crowd of excited and tipsy colleagues back into my office.

"Leo, hey."

"Babe, how did the case go?"

"I won," I breathe happily into the phone and he sighs.

"I told you ... you had absolutely nothing to worry about. You're the most persuasive person I know."

"Yeah, yeah," I twist a button between my fingers, "I'm just glad it's over."

"Me too," he shifts on the other end of the phone, "when are you coming home?"

"Soon, they're throwing a little celebration for me back at the office."

"Oh, that's sweet of them."

"It is ... after that, I'm all yours."

"Great, because I have pasta, and great news as well."

"Can't wait to hear it."

"Shandy? Where are you girl?"

My coworker Yasmine called for me from the lobby, and I turn towards the door.

"Uh – I've got to go … I'll see you soon, okay?"

"Have fun."

My door pushes open, and Yasmine stood with her hands on her hips.

"I know you aren't hiding in here while we're celebrating you."

"I'm not," I grin, holding both hands up, "I was just calling Leo."

"Oh, couldn't wait huh? Neither would I, now come on!"

Max always went all out for his workers; it was like an unspoken rule. He enjoyed seeing us happy, said it encouraged us to push harder, and do better. I thought so too.

I could honestly say that working with him was a highlight of my life ... he simply made everything pleasant, even the most graphic, devastating cases, he seemed to ease the blow.

"Keep up the good work, Shandy, you were a beast in there!"

"Max, you've been buttering me up this entire time," I tilt my head at him, and he shrugs.

"What can I say, nothing pleases me more than seeing my lawyers do their thing."

I shake my head playfully, tucking a lock of hair behind my ear.

He stared at me for a moment longer, his drink sat idly in his hand.

Max didn't look like a lawyer, much less a law firm owner, but he was. He had a beachy vibe to him, untamed short blonde hair, ocean blue eyes and a single silver circular earring hanging from his earlobe. Times have really changed.

"I'm going to head out," I tell him, breaking our gaze as I retrieve my bag from where it sat.

"Aw, already? We're just getting started," he tipped his glass between his pink lips, and I chuckle nervously.

"Nope, I've got to get home to my fiancé."

"Ah," he leaned back quickly, and nodded, "I get it. Go home to the lucky guy, tell him the good news."

"Of course."

"But, bright and early tomorrow morning, I'll need to see you at your desk, so don't have too much fun."

"Of course," I say dryly, and he winks.

"Have a good night, *Sandy*-Shandy."

Among everyone who had their indistinct chatter, Max stood out. I watched as he retreated, staring at his wide muscular back no longer covered by his blazer, but instead by a thin white button up.

I raise my index finger, touch my lips, and throw my bag over my shoulder.

When I pushed open the wooden door, I expected to see Leo at his desk, where he usually remained.

Surprisingly, he wasn't there. He was in the kitchen.

"I thought when you mentioned pasta, you meant from a restaurant," I called as I place my bag on one of our dining chairs.

"Oh, I did."

Leo meets me in between the kitchen and the dining room, and we smile at each other. With a gentle kiss, we give our nightly greetings.

"Congratulations, my love," he says as he embraces me in a tight hug, and I lay my head on his shoulder.

"Thank you."

We pull away, and he takes out a chair, encouraging me to sit.

"So, what is this big news that you've got to tell me?"

"Hold your horses," he sets the food onto the table, "let's breathe first."

I roll my eyes at his dramatics, but the smell of food immediately took up any annoyance that was brewing.

We sit, say grace, and he places the food onto our plates.

"Where'd you buy this?"

"Panada's Kitchen," he replies, and I nod.

"I've been meaning to try their food, it smells really good."

"It does."

Silence falls in between us, and I wrap the pasta around my fork, placing it into my mouth. *Fuck,* it tasted even better than it smelled. I closed my eyes, and didn't even bother covering my moan.

"Shandy," Leo called from the other side, and I open my eyes with a cheesy smile, looking forward to seeing a replica, instead, he seemed upset, "that's not ladylike, please."

"Ladylike? Leo, we're having dinner in our own home, relax."

He clears his throat, looking down at his plate. Confusedly, I continue eating, but just to save myself from further scrutiny, I eat *properly.*

"I got a promotion at work," he finally confesses, and my mouth falls open.

"Leo? That's – that's awesome. Congratulations!"

He grins in response, nodding.

"I was elated myself when I heard the news."

"Why wouldn't you be?" I was so excited, I didn't even want to eat anymore, "I'm so happy for you."

This was perfect. With a wedding not too far away, and so many plans for our future, a promotion was definitely a step in the right direction. And having won this case, I was extremely happy by how things were rolling.

"Yeah, well I'm glad you're so supportive, because we're going to have to move for the job."

Leo continued eating, but my smile faltered.

"What? What do you mean? Another state or?"

"No, it's a bit more thrilling than that, we're going to Cuba," he confesses, and my blood runs cold, "they're asking me to open another branch there, *its* ... this is huge."

"Uh—but that's … that's all the way across the world, Leo," my eyebrows furrowed in confusion, "and you made this decision on your own? You didn't even consult me?"

"Well, as my future wife, I thought you'd be fine with it? You're supposed to love and appreciate me, and trust that everything I do is to secure our future." Leo's face dropped with disappointment, and I swallow hard, shaking my head. "After everything I've done for you … I expected you to be willing to do this for me …"

Everything he's done for me? I thought displeased. Leo has always been a chivalrous guy, sometimes a little old-fashioned, but this *'wife must follow the husband'* nonsense was taking his attributes a little too far. "I—I'm not saying that I wouldn't have agreed … I'm saying it should've been a conversation."

"I apologize, love, it won't happen again," he reaches out to rub my hands, and I resist the urge to pull them from him, "but look on the bright side, in a month, we'll be somewhere else, living our best lives. Yeah?"

With a lump in my throat, I plaster on a smile, and nod weakly. "Yeah …"

two

LEO WORKED REMOTELY. He did research for different companies under a tier corporation and it has always paid well. I would understand why they'd need him to travel ... but Cuba was pretty far. The language would be different, the culture, climate—*everything*. And he just expected me to uproot my entire life to join him on his endeavor?

I woke up early the next day to head to work, because frankly, I couldn't remain in the same room with him. I completely closed up and ... he hardly noticed. He never did.

. . .

The wind was harsh and cold as I stepped into the office, shutting the door behind me.

I clip my jacket closer to my chest, my bag hanging from my fingertips, and Max pokes out his head from his office as he heard my heels click against the tiles.

"Shandy?"

He seemed a bit confused by my early arrival, and I plaster a tight-lipped smile. "Hey Max."

"It's not even 8 o'clock, what're you doing here so early?"

"Well, after my victorious win yesterday, I feel like I should prepare for the next one."

"Really," Max stepped out fully from his office, his tall, muscular build stretching along his satin blue button up, "I thought for sure you'd come in a bit later. You never cease to surprise me."

I force a small giggle, looking down at my feet.

"Gotta keep you on your toes," I shrug, "I'm gonna head to my office."

"Yeah, sure," Max stepped away, tapping a rolled up book in his palm, "you look beautiful this morning by the way, are you okay?"

"Oh—uh," I pause for a moment, my lips parting in surprise, "thank you … I'm fine, thanks."

"Of course …"

I smile at him once more, before strolling through the empty lobby, and into my office.

Blowing out a heavy breath, I plop onto my seat, rubbing my forehead. Leo's bomb last night prevented me from celebrating everything, I keep forgetting that I won a huge case just yesterday, and that I should still be in a triumphant mode.

"Here's your next case," I jump, removing my hand from my forehead as Max stood over me, "did I startle you?"

"It's fine," I brush it off, "I thought I already had my next case?"

"I upgraded you," Max says, blasé. "Seeing how good you were yesterday meant that you could fry bigger fishes."

Fuck.

Maybe if last night had a different outcome I'd be a lot more thrilled, but right now I wasn't in the right frame of mind. "Oh ... okay, that's—that's great, thank you."

I took the file from his hands, and he continued to look at me, his eyes furrowed.

"Something's off with you today."

"I'm just tired, Max," I swallow hard, raising my shoulders and trying to seem nonchalant by swinging in my chair.

"Join me for dinner after work."

"What? No, I can't—"

"It isn't a question, it's a statement. We need to discuss business."

Max leaves my office, without any room for discussion and I take a deep breath, sagging in my seat.

"Are you cold?"

"I've got my jacket," Max helps me into my coat, whilst holding my bag in the other hand.

The office was pretty quiet throughout the day, and a few people stopped by to congratulate me. It helped with lifting my spirits.

Max held up on his words and fetched me for dinner. We were taking his car since I usually took Ubers, and I wasn't exactly sure where we were going, but I knew it was somewhere nice.

Max loved expensive food.

After I took my bag from him, he helped me into his car by opening up the door, and we drove off.

The restaurant he chose wasn't too far from my home, and I silently hoped Leo wouldn't be walking past since Max chose a window seat.

"So ... what's this business we need to discuss?"

"Straight to the point, huh?" He tilts his head, waving the waiter over, "Not even a bit of conversation first?"

"I think idle conversation would make this a date ... and I can't be on a date because—"

"Since when does idle conversation equal a date? What happened to friendship?"

Embarrassment crawled up my spine and I sigh.

"You're right, I'm sorry."

"Ah, now you're making me feel bad," he leans back, looking down at me through his thick, long eyelashes, "Don't apologize."

My eyes drop to his pink, wet lips, and I quickly look away as the waiter arrives.

Max orders a bottle of wine firstly, then food.

"I don't want anything," Max narrows his eyes at me.

"Bring us the creamy cheese shrimp, with a few garlic sticks."

The man nods, and leaves. Max stares at me.

"It's great, trust me," he pours his wine into his glass, and then into mine, "You've worked for me for over six months, Shandy, why are you so ... uneasy?"

"I just have places to be, Mr. Fenton."

"One night shouldn't do any harm," he smirks, tipping the glass against his lips, "I'm sure we'll enjoy each other's company."

I purse my lips, eyeing the way his glass remained still in his hands without a tremble. He did everything so eloquently. *I'll allow it,* I thought. Besides, Leo wasn't exactly enjoyable companionship tonight, so I would kill someone for the time here.

"So then I assume there's no business to speak about," I poke, raising an eyebrow, and Max shrugs, his eyes low as he stares at me from under his long, thick eyelashes.

"You got me," he murmurs, "We're just here to enjoy dinner."

I shake my head at him amusedly, before leaning back in my chair, and crossing my legs.

"Fine."

three

"OKAY, I ADMIT," I chuckle, feeling loose and free, "The shrimp is out of this world."

"And to think you were about to let it pass by," he scoffs, "Good thing I was here to save you."

"Right," I twist my lips, trying to hold my smile, "My *superhero*."

Max offers a cheeky grin, and I chuckle under my breath, laying back calmly.

"Now, how have you been genuinely, Shandy?"

"Well—"

"And remember I said *genuinely*, you know me, Shandy, I'm a man who appreciates honesty."

I swallow hard, fumbling with the napkin at my fingertips.

"I think I'm doing well, Mr. Fenton."

"You think," he raises an eyebrow, "Is it anything I can help with?"

"Is what?"

"Whatever it is that has you unsure about how you feel."

"Oh—oh no, I—it's nothing."

"Hmm," he hums unconvinced, ushering the waitress over so she can take our plates, and I assumed we were leaving. However when I reached for my bag, he ordered dessert.

"Are you in a rush?"

He glances at me, and I reluctantly shake my head.

"Great, because I wanted to know how you felt about the win," he leans forward on his knuckle, "You left so abruptly, I didn't get a taste of how you really felt."

"It's thrilling," I admit, "The feeling is

unexplainable, and the rush—I need to feel it again."

"Wow," he breathes, a look of admiration in his eyes, "I like that you're sure about that," he chuckles, and I merely smile.

"I should then assume that you're on board for the next case? Did you look it over?"

"I did."

"And?"

I blow out a breath, dropping my head lightly from side to side.

"It's a tricky one ... there's a lot of evidence against her."

"There is," he shrugs, "Not to mention the prosecutor is a strong one, she's never lost."

Shit.

"But I trust you," Max adds on, "That's why I gave it to you."

I'm not sure I even trust myself that much.

"That's also why I need you to tell me what's going on," Max takes a deep breath, his face now solemn, "My employees mean a lot to me Shandy, and I can always tell when something's off. Your mind isn't completely here, and even if you don't go in depth, I need to know what it is so I can plan accordingly."

"Plan accordingly?"

"Yes," he nods, "If I should pull the case from you, give you some time off – whatever may help your situation."

"I don't think that'll be necessary."

"Then tell me what's going on."

I eye him, my throat itchy, and my mouth dry. I didn't plan to tell him *so* soon, I thought I'd at least have some time to conjure up some sort of big, understanding explanation. But I didn't. It was here and now. "I … I may have to leave soon."

Max furrows his eyebrows, his body rigid. "Leave … where?"

"My fiancée has to move for work … and we may have to move to Cuba."

"Cuba?" Max sputters, "Is that something you want to do?"

"Well, in order for him to—"

"Is it something that *you* want to do, Shandy?"

I look down at my lap, a lump forming in my throat.

"I'm not sure just yet, b-but we're about to get married ... what other choice could I possibly have?"

Max looked at me, his lips parted, his eyes enlarged, "You always have a choice, Shandy. You could just stay here and continue to build your life. You've got a great personality, a great job, you don't need ... you can just do so much more for yourself here."

"I know, but—"

"But what?" He rejoined. "People are escaping these countries to find refuge here, and you're going to run over to the country they're running from?"

"It won't be like that," I tell him, my voice shaky as I look back up at him, and his eyes soften.

"Who are you trying to convince, me ... or you?"

I avert my eyes, unable to say anything else.

"When are the two of you supposed to leave?"

"In two months' time."

"This case calls in about a month … You have a bit of time but, can you handle it with everything you've got going on?"

"I can," I nod reassuringly, and he continues to eye me for a moment before sighing.

"Alright, if you say you can, then I believe you. Just don't fuck this up, Shandy. This isn't scheduling a hair appointment, or catering to a wedding, this is us trying to determine someone's future."

"I-I get that."

Max sighs once more, before nodding.

He refills his glass of wine, and I drum my fingers against the table.

"Nevertheless, I do hope that you make the right decision."

The right, decision. What would that be?

Max dropped me off at home after spending the next 30 minutes trying to cheer me up. It worked. Or maybe it was just the wine, but I was a giggling mess.

I always enjoyed his company, it was just all around good energy, and smiles when it needed to be. He would never let there be a dull moment.

"I'll see you at the office on Monday, have the weekend off."

"Max – you don't need to do that."

"I want to. Monday morning I expect you to be at your best."

I stand outside of his window, holding my bag in front of me. "Okay," I murmur with a nod, and he smiles.

"Have a good night, Shandy."

I nod, before turning to head into my house. He waits until I shut the door behind me before he leaves, and I gingerly smile to myself as I shut the door.

The house was left in complete darkness, and I assumed that Leo was just asleep.

I peeled off my heels, and sighed, turning on the lights to the kitchen. As I gulped a bottle of water, enjoying the feeling of it sliding down my throat after an entire night of wine drinking, I concluded that it's been a while since I've had a good night. And I'll give Max his props for that.

four

WHEN I SLIPPED into bed as quietly as I could, I noticed that Leo was turned away from me. I didn't question it, perhaps he just fell asleep that way. I shut off my lamp, and went to bed. And boy was it peaceful.

When we woke up together the next morning, he hardly acknowledged me, and that's when I knew something was up. In the bathroom, I stood naked in front of him, and he turned away ... and pretended I didn't exist.

He disappeared into the kitchen, leaving me upstairs while I checked some things on my email. I pad downstairs, the frying pan sizzling on the stove.

Enough was enough...

"Hey ... is something wrong?" I rubbed my elbow as I walked towards him, slowly climbing onto the stool.

"We have lunch with my parents," he tells me, ignoring my question and hardly looking up. I furrow my eyebrows.

"I can't, I have a case to work on," I reply. The last place I wanted to be was at the mercy of his entire family while he watched me get eaten alive.

"We won't stay long then," he says, shrugging his shoulder and I bite the inside of my cheek. I watch as he scrambled his eggs, throwing in a bit of salt.

"I'll be frank then," I mutter, "I don't want to go to your parents."

"Oh, I bet you don't," he chuckles humorlessly, "I know you'd rather stay out with Mr. Fenton until one o'clock in the morning."

There it is. *Shit, was it really that late?*

He dumps my plate in front of me, and I raise both eyebrows. "If you have something to say, Leo, just say it," I scoff.

"Don't tell me what to do as if you're not the one in trouble here," he snarls, "Where were you?"

"I'm going to need you to dial it down," my forehead creases in confusion, "In trouble? Who's in trouble because it's not me?"

Leo continues to make his breakfast. His face stoic, and angry.

"I have a new case—I remained after work with Max to work on it."

"Until one o'clock in the morning? That's not weird at all."

"Are you also forgetting that I'm a grown woman," I gape, "we spent more time on it than we anticipated. A lot of my cases from here on out are going to require a lot more of my attention ... are you going to react this way every time it does?"

"Thank goodness I won't have to deal with this shit much longer," he says, scooping up some eggs and stuffing them into his mouth.

I close my mouth. I wanted to retort, but I needed to pick my battles.

"Hm," he huffs, shaking his head, "Just be dressed in ten minutes."

"Ten minutes? Now you're being ridiculous," I stand from where I sat, "I said I couldn't make it, and that's that. Please give everyone greetings on my behalf."

I leave my plate on the table, and storm to my home office, shutting the door behind me.

I bet he'd love to take me to his family, so that he could calmly complain about how I *behaved*, then bask in all of their praises about how good of a man he was. Well, *no thanks*, I'd much rather work on and try to get somewhere in this case. I wanted to put my all into it, and that's exactly what I'll do.

He didn't bother me, nor press the issue, instead I heard his car squealing out of the driveway and I rolled my eyes in response.

Pulling the files out of my drawer and trying to focus, only proved that Leo was still going to have an effect on me, even while he's not here. I knew he would have something to say, and I would've been okay with that if it didn't seem like he was a father correcting his daughter.

· · ·

This case was a gruesome one, and I knew it would need all of my attention, but I kept rereading every line trying to put two and two together. I couldn't do it right now.

My phone rang, and I sighed thinking it was Leo, but instead Max's name displayed across the screen.

"Max? Is something wrong?"

"Is this how you answer the phone with everyone? Seems a little negative if you ask me."

I chuckle, leaning back in my chair. "This is not, in fact, how I answer the phone with everyone, you're just ... you know."

"I know, I'm not accustomed to calling," he chuckles.

"Exactly, *but* I wanted to check in, and ensure that you were alright."

"Oh ..." I play with the gentle fabric of my shirt, "I'm doing okay, thank you."

"Uh ... do you have lunch – or would you like to grab some lunch?"

Grab ... some lunch?

I stare at my computer screen, and then the files displayed across my desk ... *I should stay and get this done – that's what I should tell Leo. But I couldn't focus right now, so it would be pointless, wouldn't it?*

"Uh ... s-sure," I reply softly, still a bit hesitant.

"Great, I'll pick you up in thirty."

"Okay."

As we hang up, I freeze, staring at my computer screen. *Oh boy, did I just agree to lunch with my boss? While my fiancé nearly exploded by the thought of me out with another man?*

"Where would you like to eat?"

Max was dressed casually, which wasn't a first, but I hadn't noticed just how good he looked without his suit and tie as well. Not saying I don't prefer a man in his suit, but still.

His hair was covered with a baseball hat, and that allowed the shape of his face to be highlighted.

"I'm not sure," I ponder, "I'm craving greasy food."

"Fast food then?"

"Thin salty fries, and burgers."

Max chuckles, shaking his head.

"Your wish is my command," he replies, and I grin.

We find a nearby McDonalds, and he places our orders, and hands me my food.

"We need to find a spot to eat," he murmurs more to himself while I sit in the passenger side happily.

I may be in trouble when I get home, but for now, I was living my best life.

five

"WHAT MADE you ask me to lunch?"

"Well, I was actually just leaving the office," he explains, "one of my cases are proving to be a lot more difficult than I anticipated."

"How so?"

Max finds a nearby beach, and parks, allowing us to sit in the A/C as we eat. I didn't complain, it was a calming place.

"Well, a woman stabbed and killed her son."

I gape.

"In self-defense."

"Self-defense?" I ask, alarmed.

"Allegedly, she says she woke up to her son choking her, so she reached for the knife on the side of her bed, and stabbed him two times."

"Oh," I frown, my appetite decreasing, "Do you believe her?

Max sighs, looking out through his windshield and out at the ocean.

"I want to ..." he confesses, "But there's just ... something she isn't telling me."

"I'm sure you'll get it ... you're the best of the best," I remark, shoving a french-fry into my mouth.

He chuckles, glancing over at me. "Am I?"

"You are," I nod, and he shrugs.

"As long as you're saying it, I have no choice but to believe."

"Real cheesy," I joke, and he narrows his eyes at me. I continue eating, the cold milkshake raising goosebumps on my skin as the A/C blows.

"So ... if you don't mind me asking, have you made your decision?"

"It's been one day, Max," I pause with another fry in my mouth.

"You're right," he raises both hands, "you can't blame me. After your revelation, I'm worried about one of my best lawyers, leaving."

"I won one criminal case," I chuckle.

"Don't try to downplay it, you gave it your all, and you understood the importance of it. Then you got up, and you did everything you could. *Your very first case,* and the judge was completely in your favor. That's something to hang on your wall."

As Max praises me, I can't help but smile. It's not often that my accomplishments are dwelled upon, but when they are, it's an indescribable feeling.

"Which is why I hope that you stay. You have so much potential, Shandy, I ... I hope that you see it. You can do so much here, build a stable life that suits *you, and your needs.* You can be great."

Max was right about certain things, but when it all came down to it, Leo was my fiancé ... he's done so much for me, and I feel like the least I could do was be there for him ... even if it meant uprooting my life here to travel across the world so that he could follow his dreams.

"I can see that this is a bit depressing for you, so I won't mention it again," Max says, "I trust that whatever decision you make, it'll be because you wholeheartedly wanted to. "Now come on," Max steps out of the vehicle, walks over and opens my door. I put all of my trash together, and reluctantly take his outstretched hands. "I won't bite," he chuckles, and I nervously let him lead me onto the beach.

The sand was a bit hot, seeping between my toes as I walked, and the sounds of the ocean filled all over the silence in the air.

Max glances at me a few times, before settling for the ocean.

"You're just as beautiful as this view," he compliments, and I choke up.

"Uh – t-thank you?"

He shrugs. "I'm only stating the obvious," Max removes his cap with his other hand, and his hair lifts to life, "When's the last time you've been to the beach?"

"Honestly, it's been a long time," I admit, taking a small glance around, "I've forgotten what it feels like … what it smells like …"

"We're often so wrapped up in our own little world's … that we don't notice the smaller things, we forget about all the things that made us whole."

I glanced at Max, who seemed to be in his own world. He was reminiscing, I could see it all over his face. I decide to remain quiet, and let him relive whatever memory he was enjoying right now.

As for me, I just appreciated the breeze as it blew against my skin. I wanted to forget, while he remembered.

After the beach, Max and I grabbed some cake from the Dough Factory, and drove around jamming to his favorite tunes. Surprisingly, his playlist didn't differ much from mine.

"I should get you home," he says, as we glance at the time on his dash board, "Not that I want to but, you know."

"Stop it," I shake my head at him, as if disapprovingly, when really all I wanted to say is that I can stay. *But I couldn't, I really, really couldn't. Awe shit, what the heck was happening?* In a blink of an eye, a wonderful morning morphed into some kind of first date filled with promise and curiosity. I was giddy, elated, floating on a cloud...

As six-thirty blinked, I realized how fast time went by when we were together. I also wondered if Leo was home. Dread immediately settled in my stomach, and I realized that I hadn't thought of him much while I was hanging with Max.

'Hearts of fire
Creates love desire
Take you high and higher
To the world you belong..."

Earth, Wind & Fire play on the stereo, and I lean against the car door. Max drove me home, not saying anything much, we just settled in our silence ... and I was okay with that. I found comfort in being with him, I figured that out today, and whether it was from him being such an authority figure in my life ... or maybe just him being a friend, I was grateful for it.

We slowed to a stop.

"Tell your fiancé, I'm sorry for stealing you today," Max jokes, and I laughed, but really my body felt hot with anxiety.

"Thanks for today, Max ... I didn't even know I needed it."

"Anytime, Shandy. I'll see you on Monday."

I nod, and stand outside as he leaves. I turn towards my house, and I sigh as I notice Leo's car in the driveway.

Here we go.

six

MAXWELL FENTON, ATTORNEY AT LAW

TRUTH BE TOLD, the beach always reminds me of my mother. She died when I was fourteen, and her dying wish was to be cremated and her ashes thrown across the ocean.

The waves crashing against the shore always reminds me of her and the way she used to pick me up when I was a little boy and swing me around and around, my legs slicing through the air and the ocean breeze just above the water.

I loved my mom, and I miss her dearly. She would be proud of my accomplishments now, owning and running my own defense firm. She always wanted me to be a lawyer, and I always did like the law.

It's always preferable to want to root and be on the winning side of the law, I thought about becoming a prosecutor, but then that little voice inside me liked the challenge. Don't the *accused* need good legal representation too? It was an opposition I was willing to fight for.

Not Guilty

My two favorite words.

As I drive back from the beach, I think about my lonely house. At thirty-something, I should have been married by now, had a few kids, or at least a dog or cat. But all that awaits me now is my sprawling mansion on the mountain-top, cold marble floors and an 85-inch Roku TV.

Maybe I'll watch Netflix for awhile, maybe not. What's on Amazon Prime? The same ole—same ole.

FUCK ME!

Why can't I get her outta my head?!

From the moment she walked into my office for a job interview I was mesmerized.

It was six months ago that I hired her. She was a tall, chestnut skin beauty, with shoulder length black hair, dark eyes and pink lips. Straight white teeth, I always try to get her to smile—I love to see her smile!

My heart skips a beat every time she enters a room. My eyes always seem to search for her whenever we're in a crowd—*what the hell was happening to me?!* I've never had a crush per se on any woman, but with Shandy—I've got it bad.

There was just one little obstacle ... she was taken.

And, I mean, *really* taken—not just a boyfriend, but a fiancé. She was promised to be married and I take that commitment seriously. I honor devotion, being faithful and true.

So I've tried to find little reasons to steal her attention away, even if it meant it was a work-related purpose. Breakfast meetings, lunch, even dinner to talk about a case. What case? Any case ... Whatever the rationality, no personal conversation should come up ...

Until lately.

Now, it's all I want to talk about! To get to know her. What makes her tick? What was she like as a little girl?

But lately...

She doesn't appear to be happy, *why?*

She walks into the office now staring at her shoes, *why?*

She has a faraway look on her face, *why?*

Why? Why? Why?

What is going on with her?!

I try repeatedly to reach her, but can't seem to break that barrier between work and intimacy.

I know she's attracted to me, I've noticed her once or twice searching for my locale too. Seen her glance away from occasionally staring my way, even caught her dropping her eyes to my lips.

I want to kiss her too.

Am I wrong in reading the signs?

Was it all wishful thinking?

seven

SHANDY

THE MOMENT I step into the house, I already feel the hostility. The chopping board echoed through the hall, and I shut my eyes tight as I place my bag on the dining table.

"Leo?" I call loudly, just to ease the air although I knew he was there.

Leo stood in the kitchen, cutting carrots.

"Hey," I murmur, "how was lunch?"

"It was good, thanks," he said pleasantly, not looking up at me, "You were missed."

I gulp, walking closer to the island. "Oh," I bite the

inside of my cheek, "I'm sure I'll be able to make it next time."

Leo angrily chops down on the carrot, nearly cutting his finger.

"Be careful," I warn him.

"Oh, so now you care?"

"Now I care? What are you even talking about?"

"You couldn't make it to lunch with *me*, but you could sure fit it in with your boss."

"Leo," I sigh, rubbing my forehead, "It isn't like that. We've been ... *swamped* at work. When he asked me out to lunch, I knew it would be to talk about cases."

"So that's what you guys did? Talk about cases?"

My heart hammered in my chest as Leo continued to slice the carrots aggressively. If he kept up at that pace, the carrots would be drizzled with blood.

"Yes, that's all."

"You know, it's almost as if we're not supposed to get married soon. You should've shown all the lies and deceit in the dating stage."

"I - I'm not lying to you, Leo. I know how it looks, but you know how your parents are around me."

"They love you," he says, and I stare at him incredulously.

"No they don't, Leo," I chuckle humorlessly, "My week has been difficult enough, the last thing I need right now is your mother subtly calling me fat, and your aunties telling me I'm getting too old so I need to make a child."

Leo finally calms down, placing the knife on the counter. "Why don't you talk to me anymore?"

Because you don't talk to me either—you just dictate—and growl every time something doesn't go your way. "I'm sorry," I frown, "I ... I just have a lot going on."

He sighs, walking around the table. He wraps his arms around me.

"We're a team, Shandy, you know that, if there's anything bothering you, I should be the first to know."

"I'll always help you in any way that I can ..." I sigh, nodding, "I know that."

"Great," he pulls away, lifting my chin so that he could place a kiss onto it. "And I trust you ... but just ... Maybe just stop going out with your boss."

"It's not like that—"

"I'm telling you what to do, it's just that I'm sure you want what's best for our relationship, and this is what's best."

Right.

I swallow hard, plastering a smile on my face. "Sure, hun, whatever makes you happy."

Monday came around quick, with Sunday being filled with household chores like washing, and cleaning. Leo settled for a day with his boys, and if I'm being completely honest, I wasn't disappointed.

The alone time was much needed – well – after I pondered a hundred times over whether I should call Max or not, but I decided against it. He was my boss, and I had already told Leo that I would've stop all of the extra-curricular activities with him.

As I got ready for work, I noted that Leo was already up.

"You're up early," I mutter surprised and he smiles.

"Good morning to you too," he leans over to place a kiss on my cheek, and hands me my Spanx so that I could slip into my dress.

I was shocked, but nevertheless I pull on my clothes. He helped me throughout the entire process, strapping my shoes, handing me my hair brushes, even grabbing my water out of the fridge.

"Have a great day, love," he says as I leave.

"You as well," we place a small kiss on each other's lips as I leave with the Uber waiting for me.

Leo's not accustomed to behaving this way, but I wasn't going to complain. I wasn't sure how to react to it all, but I only hoped that it would last for a long time.

I don't know what changed.

When I got to work, my spirits were raised to the roof. I had forgotten about everything else for the while, and decided to focus on good that was happening now.

However, I found Max in my office.

"Max?"

"Good morning," he greets, his voice still raspy as if he had just gotten up, "You look beautiful this morning."

Once again my breath clogs in my throat, and I manually swallow so that I don't squeak like a mouse.

"Max, it's too early for your pleasantries."

"Well, I wish I could dwell on them, really, but we may have a problem."

I furrow my eyebrows, slowly walking towards my desk as he stands and huffs.

"There's a slight change to your case," he admits.

"Change," I tilt my head at him curiously, "what change?"

"The judge moved the hearing to next week."

My eyes widen, "Next week??"

He nods in response, running a hand through his slick hair.

"We've got to get on it," he says, "like now."

"O- of course, *shit* – um – let me just," I place my bag on the table, pulling out the file.

"I know this may be a bit abrupt for you, so I'll remain to help you."

"Thanks," I breathe a sigh of relief, but it's short-lived. Presenting a case in less than 30 days was a risk, but in less than 7 days? *That's suicide.*

We go over everything, and try to find any loopholes that we could, but it was difficult. By lunch time, I had removed my blazer feeling hot flashes all over my skin. I couldn't lose my second case, it was just as important as the first, and all of the others that would eventually come.

Max leaned back in his chair, his pen between his lips as he stared at some of the evidence. My eyes linger a bit, but I don't let him see.

He was focused, which is what I should be, but his long legs stretch across the room, clothed in firmly fitting black pants, and a hint of his tattoo ran into the cuff of his shirt.

To end my eyeing session, my door pushes open, and to my surprise, Leo stood before the two of us.

My eyes widen, and I part my lips as the two men stare at each other.

"Uh ... good afternoon," Leo clears his throat, a paper bag in his hands. He looks between Max and I, and thankfully, we weren't sitting together.

"Leo? What're you doing here?"

"I came to bring you lunch."

He places the paper bag on the table awkwardly, and I stand.

"That's ... sweet of you. Thanks."

"What's going on here?" He asks, a smile on his face as he feigned genuine curiosity.

"Just ... working."

I didn't want to be rude or brisk, but he should know he can't just barge into my office, and then question me about my work, in front of my boss. He's never brought me lunch before, so this wasn't something I could fully fathom.

We just stood there, staring at each other while Max tried to mind his business.

"Yup," he rocked on his heel, "That's all. I'll see you at home."

"Yeah," I nod.

"At … 4? 5?"

"Whenever I'm done, Leo."

"Right," he glances at Max curtly before he leaves, and I sigh.

"I'm sorry, I'm sure you know he's never done this before."

"It's alright," Max waves me off, "He's doing a good thing taking care of his fiancée, and you deserve nothing less."

I laugh shortly, rubbing the back of my neck, and returning to analyzing the files. Max honestly didn't seem too bothered by it, and I was grateful that he didn't make it any more awkward.

SEVEN O'CLOCK IN THE EVENING

"...I DON'T KNOW."

As I rubbed my forehead, Max runs a hand over his face.

"I need to do a deep dive," Max says, "and *you* need to rest."

"What? No, this is my case, I should—"

"Get some rest," he repeats, "we'll pick this back up tomorrow morning."

Max hands me my coat, and I sigh exasperatedly, as we both stand.

"Come on, I'll give you a ride home."

We need a breakthrough on this case, or else our client will be going to jail. When we got onto the highway, there was intense traffic.

"While we're sitting here, we can continue to look into it," I suggest, and Max sighs.

"Your brain needs a rest, Shandy."

"How are you so calm about this?"

"I know I'll get through," he says, "and you? I have faith in you ... With you and I working on the case, we'll be fine."

I wish I had that much faith in myself.

"We can pass the time another way," Max grins, and I tilt my head at him.

Why did that sound so sexual? "And what way would that be?"

"Let's get to know each other."

"Really?" I couldn't control the burst of laughter that escaped and he purses his lips at me.

"What's so funny about that?"

The vehicle moves forward every ten minutes, and I shrug, "It's just that you're my boss."

"Yeah, and?"

"And..." My mouth closes shut. *Why was I fighting so hard not to get to know him? He was interesting enough, a nice person, pleasant on the eyes, even a great boss.* "You should get to know *me* first." I stare at the side of his face and my eyes lower to his throat. I felt the urge to run my lips across his skin and I adjust the position in my seat.

"Hmmm," he lets go, grinning. "What do I *not* know about Shandy Johnson?"

I shyly gaze out the window and at the car next to us. "I mean I know *you* were one of the top students in law school."

"True," he admits, "and I know *you* volunteered at a dog shelter about two years ago."

I smile, *I miss those dogs...* I shift in my car seat again, only this time, my legs angle towards his body, "I know you've been single for awhile."

He glances the other way, his hands still on the steering wheel, "And how do you know that?"

"Girls in the office like to gossip," I make him smile. He has a nice grin. His reaction sparks butterflies in my stomach. *I want to touch him so badly...*

We start to pick up a little speed. "I know you've been written up for reckless driving numerous times, that's why you take an Uber."

"Wow," I deadpan, "was the license part really necessary?"

We both laugh, "You can't blame me for the fact that you can't drive."

"Hey, I can drive!" I guffaw, "I just ... don't like driving like a snail."

"Right, you've got a need for speed," he continues to poke fun, and I can't help but giggle at almost everything he says. It's not that it was all very funny, it's that he made them sound so hilarious.

"Alright then, ask me what you'd like to know, I'll answer honestly." I brace for personal questions.

"Tell me about your childhood."

"My childhood," I raise my eyes to the car roof in wonder, "okay uh ... I grew up in a small town in Wisconsin. My parents were very lovely people. A bit shy, and naïve, but I guess I can't blame them. They were teen parents … nevertheless, they were amazing."

"I'm actually really glad to hear that," Max says.

"Really, why?"

"Because … it's not often that you hear a … normal childhood. You're often met with abuse … or some sort of trauma—"

"Is it because I'm black?"

Max seemed a bit taken aback by my question, and glances over at me.

"You're being serious? Of course not. It's based on what I've heard myself. In case you forgot … I'm a lawyer. I hear these things for a living."

"You're right," I shut my eyes in embarrassment, "I'm sorry—I don't—I don't know what I was thinking."

"I guess it's a valid question," he says, "nothing to be ashamed of, I was just surprised."

"I-it's not even that I was offended, I was just—uh —genuinely curious."

"I'm an idiot, and that's all there is to it," he says, and looks over his shoulder to make a lane change.

"Tell me about *your* childhood," I desperately wanted to escape my shame.

"Uh, well, my mom died when I was fourteen, and I basically lived with a single dad until he remarried ten years later. By that time, I was already in college and out of the house."

"I'm sorry," I tell him, realizing that I might have brought up a sore subject.

He sighs, "She liked the beach, and so did I."

That's what he was thinking of at the beach the other day. His mother...

My heart felt heavy for him, growing up without a mother. I knew his pain. "My parents passed a few years ago, they died together."

I think I may have shocked him. He whips his head around, "How?"

"They went on vacation ... the boat sank, and they drowned."

"Fuck ..." Max whispered.

"I find comfort in imagining them passing together, in each other's arms. I think it's much better than dying alone."

"Is that something you're afraid of? Dying alone?"

I pause for a moment, playing with a loose thread on my skirt. "Perhaps ... it is."

"Can I ask you another question, Shandy? You don't have to answer, but I ... it's been bothering me."

Another lane change and we're off the freeway.

"Go ahead."

"Why do you feel like you need to go to Cuba with Leo? I get that he's your fiancé, and maybe you do love him unconditionally, but that's not the vibe I get."

I expected that question. It was something I asked myself often. Something I fooled myself with ... *Why did I feel like I needed to?* "When I graduated high school, my parents passed soon after," I began, staring at the mat underneath my feet, "I met Leo at a grief support group I went to, he had just lost his grandmother ... we ... we bloomed from there."

"Like a survivor's group?" He asks, now at the stop light.

"Yes, at first it was amazing. Date nights, trips, gifts, he was this … perfect man, and he came at a time where I … I needed *someone*. But then it was time to get serious, his parents were wealthy, they knew people. They helped me get into one of the best schools, and they paid for every single thing."

Max began to nod his head.

In the corner of my eye, I can see him listen to me tentatively. "They helped with our mortgage when I graduated and decided that Leo and I was doing well enough to settle, and well, they never fail to remind me of that up to this day. Neither does he."

"So, wait, you're doing all of this, because they helped you?"

"Max—"

"No," Max scoffs, "they can't hold what they did over your head as if you forced them to do it. You don't owe these people a thing, a thank you, maybe, but definitely not your life."

"It's not that simple—"

"It *is* that simple. And I think you know the answer, so I'm going to ask again."

Max parks his car in the middle of the road and turns to stare at me.

"Do *you* want to go to Cuba?"

nine

"Do you want to go to Cuba, Shandy?"

MY BRAIN FELT like a record player. Going on, and on, and on. I knew the answer, I really did, but how would I tell Leo?

When Max dropped me off, he was hesitant. I could tell there was so much more that he wanted to say, but I couldn't stick around for it.

I felt like we had crossed a boundary, like our relationship was becoming a lot more than what it should be, and my conscience couldn't take that right now. Because then Leo would be right, he would have yet another thing to hold above my head.

The truth is, I loved Leo because he saved me, but when he dropped that bomb on me a few weeks ago, without even considering me, I couldn't help but feel the distance between us.

Leo's car parked in the driveway made me anxious, and nowadays, it always did.

I asked Max to drop me off before at the driveway, I knew Leo would be watching.

He told me to call him if anything, but right now I wasn't even sure that I'd be back at work. This was quickly going downhill.

I stepped into the house, and as soon as I shut the door, a hand clamped around my throat.

I yelp in surprise, shutting my eyes tightly as I'm slammed against the wall.

"It's nine o'clock, Shandy," Leo growls, and I try to gasp for air, "My patience has running thin."

"L-L-LEO?"

I try to get him to release me, but he's strong. *What is he doing?* Fear ran up my spine at the thought of him ... attacking me? I couldn't believe that this was real!

"I was going to try, Shandy," he says, "I was going to try to be better for you, but you know what, you don't *want* better!"

He lets me go roughly, and I fall onto my knees, my eyes wide with fear as I desperately inhale, staring at the floor.

"This is what you want, isn't it? After all my family have done for you—*bitch,* this is how you repay us?"

"What the hell is wrong with you?" I croak, once I found my voice and he scoffs. "Why are you so jealous all of a sudden?"

"Jealous?" He spits. "You're the one fucking your boss!"

"You don't even know what you're talking about!" I drag away from him, using the edge of the couch to help me stand, "I'm not sleeping with anyone but you."

"You're a whore Shandy, I don't know what changed, but you—*you,*" Leo laughs manically, pacing back and forth. "You know I won't let you embarrass me. I could see it all over your face when I brought you lunch. And he just sat there like a smug motherfucker, knowing that he's already had his way with you."

"You're delusional," I tell him, turning to head up the stairs.

"Where the fuck do you think you're going?"

He chased after me, and my heart echoed loudly in my chest as I ran through the hall into our bedroom. I slam the door, and lock it, stepping away so that I could find something to protect myself with.

Leo has never laid a hand on me, *ever*. Maybe he's spoken to me roughly once or twice, maybe he's been aggressive with things in the house, but he's never … he's *never* touched me like this. His reaction scares me. I'm scared to death! Tears brim my eyes, and I run a hand through my hair as he hollers and screams from behind the door like a rabid dog.

My phone was left downstairs, and there was nothing that I could find in this moment that would help me in anyway.

"Leo you need to calm down!" I yell, "y-you're scaring me." The banging on the door stops, and although my breath was jagged and uneven, I try to remain calm. "L-let's just have a conversation, babe, let's talk about it."

"Let's talk about it," his voice was hoarse, and it made me extremely reluctant, but staying in here wouldn't do me any good.

I slowly open the door, my hands trembling. He stands away from it opening, watching my every movement as I let him in.

"I'm sorry for putting my hands ... on you," he murmurs and I gulp, "you just – it makes me so mad ... the thought of sharing you with someone else ... I can't stand it."

He walks slowly towards me, and I resist the urge to step away. He places a hand on my cheek, and I try my best to lean into his touch without flinching.

"You should quit ..."

My entire body froze, "What?"

"He's going to get in between us, Shandy, I know it. I can support the both of us—"

"Quit? I've worked so hard for this—"

"You can find something in Cuba—"

"I'm not going to fucking Cuba!" I snarl, rage building up within me.

Leo's eye twitches, "Excuse me?"

"I said," I clench my fists, "I'm not going to Cuba."

"You ungrateful whore," he spits, and I fold my arms, "After everything we've done for you, you're going to throw it away for what? For a man that doesn't give two shits about you?"

"Well, he could've fooled me?" I raise both hands helplessly, letting them slap the side of my thigh. "The way he gives two shits about my life, the way he speaks to me, the way he considers me, it's a hell of a lot more than what you do."

"I put you through law school—"

"Thank you!" I scream, my chest rising and falling, "Thank you so much, Leo, for supporting my dream, just as much as I've supported yours! But this is my life to live, not yours!"

Leo's pupils were dilated, his arm practically shook with rage. I knew he was getting angry all over again, but this time I wasn't going to stick around for what he could do. "But, you're mine Shandy."

I turn to look at him, "almost yours." I left first this time, leaving him in the room. I rush downstairs, towards my bag and grab my phone to call Max. "Max, I need you to come get me, please."

"Okay," he says, with no questions asked, "I'm not far."

My phone is ripped from my hand, and thrown against the wall.

"You want to test my crazy Shandy—is this what this is?"

"It's over, Leo."

"It's over?" He scoffs, "What's over?"

"Me and you, we're not going to work out. You're moving to Cuba, and I'm—"

"Going to fuck your white boss."

I decide to wait outside, not feeling safe in my own home.

"If you leave here today Shandy, it's best that you know that you can't ever come back."

"I won't need to," I tell him, and he nods.

"You've made your decision."

It couldn't be that easy, I thought, as he watched me shut the door behind myself. I didn't stay to find out though, Max squealed to a stop, and I sprinted into his car.

"Thanks for coming," I breathe, and he nods, staring at me. I could tell that he was worried, but I was still trying to process everything that went on.

"Of course," he says, his voice laced with worry. "Are you all right?"

"I-I'm good. Don't worry about me, I just—just get me to a hotel or something."

"A hotel? You need somewhere to sleep tonight?"

"Yeah … long story."

"You can stay with me."

"No," I reply quickly, "absolutely not. You're my boss, and I don't mean to impose—"

"I think I'm a bit more than your boss since I'm here picking you up so you can get away from your fiancé."

I stay quiet, staring ahead.

"You're not staying alone tonight, I won't allow it."

Good, I thought to myself, because I'm not sure I could handle all of this by myself.

ten

MAX

AS I WATCH the hard prints form against Shandy's neck, my body stiffened in anger.

How dare he lay his hand on her? Who does he think he is? I know he thinks he's gotten away with it, but that couldn't be farther from the truth. I will make sure that he gets what is coming to him, but in the meantime, I'm just glad that Shandy was away from him. Fucker didn't even know that he pushed her right into my open arms, but he did. Thug's like him will probably demand she repay what he's invested—I've seen it before with men like him—little does he know, he's messing with the wrong defender.

Beautiful, smart, driven, Shandy just didn't know it yet. She was everything a man needed, and more.

As I watch her from a chair, she stirs away, her hair shifts with her movements. She's sleeping now in my guest bedroom, as I frown as she winces in pain, her eyes fluttering awake.

"Shit," she whispers, lifting herself off the bed, "Max?"

"Hey," I murmur quietly, "you slept for quite some time."

She hums in response, rubbing her eyes. "Have you been there all night? What time is it anyway?"

I stand to my feet. "Six o'clock in the morning."

"I'm sorry," she yawns, "I-I'm going to leave."

"No," I tell her, "I got you some fresh clothes … just refresh yourself, and come downstairs when you're ready, my housekeeper is making us some food."

"Are you sure?"

She finally opens her eyes fully, looking at me with those beautiful, brown eyes.

"I'm sure," I merely whisper, and she smiles tenderly.

"Thank you."

I let her be, closing the door gently behind me.

I saunter into the kitchen, "Mary Ann, did you make some breakfast like I asked?"

"I did, Mr. Fenton."

"Good, have everything ready in about fifteen minutes, and not a minute later."

"Yes, sir."

The door shuts upstairs, and I knew. Shandy slowly padded down the stairs, I could tell that she felt a bit sheepish. Even in my sweatpants her shape stood out, I willed myself to just stare into her eyes. It was one of her best features.

"Look at you," I tease, and she tilts her head at me, pausing warmly, "Alright, alright."

I join her at the bottom.

"We have the case to work on," she reminds me, and I nod. Even in her dullest moments, she's always ready to go.

"For now, let's eat. Then we can get to it."

"We're not going into the office?"

"No, I let Peter handle it today, we can work from home."

"Max," she frowns, "I'm fine, you know? We can—I can get to work."

"I don't doubt that," I tell her, "but I'm starving, so your workaholic self will just have to wait."

She relaxes a bit, smiling insecurely. Her phone sat in her hands, and I can't help but glance at it. *Does she want to call him? Is she waiting for a call?* "Everything will be OK," I encourage her.

"Right now," she sighs, placing it onto the table, "Everything's okay."

With her assurance, I smile. *From this point forward, no one will take advantage of her ... I'll make sure of that.*

SHANDY

Had some time to think about it last night, while I pretended to be asleep, I knew there was always this underlying issue with Leo and I—he could always be a bit of a *dick*—selfish, self-centered and narcissistic. **Me,** not **We** can describe him to a 'T'. He would have never came to me with his decision to relocate, to find out if it was a good idea for *us*—he already made up his mind. He just assumed that I would drop everything ... my career, my friends, just to follow him to Cuba? And now he's being a bully—strong-arming me into giving into his demand and forcing me to sacrifice everything that I've worked hard for? Do I really want to marry someone like that? Enter a marriage with this ultimatum hanging over my head? Asshole would probably demand all the money his parents forked over to put me through law school too. I wouldn't even put it passed him if he took me to court. *Yes, asshole...*

Took a few peeks at Max asleep on the chair beside me, and I looked deep in my heart and felt a void where there once was love. *Was I jumping out of the frying pan and into the fire?* Probably, but I didn't care ... There must have always been issues between Leo and I—it took this one moment to shake me alive. Eyes wide open in the dead of night, I look at Max Fenton, Attorney at Law, boss ... friend. With his hand and wrist propping up his tilted head, dreaming away. I now had feelings for him. *Deep feelings* ... if my heart wasn't free, I would have never have fallen ... I pause to view Max in a new light. Not only helping when I was vulnerable, but a soul mate.

I wait till his housekeeper is around the corner when I step into Max and tap him on his shoulder.

He turns around and stares down at me—I get lost in his crystal blue eyes.

We grab one another in a hug, and a warm embrace melts my constraint. I lay my head near the crux of his shoulder and envelop my arms around his backside. He's rigid and comfortable at the same time, and it felt natural to be in his arms. I hold him tight and instantly feel the release of my tears, as he instinctively cups the back of my head, reassuring me.

It felt like home.

I am home.

acknowledgments

McDonalds

Dough Factory

"That's the Way of the World"

By Earth, Wind & Fire

Roku TV

Netflix

Amazon Prime

Uber

Cynthia Parcel was a highly regarded college professor. She was a black beauty with the brains to match. Her life was on the fast-track, dreams had already come true; she was successful, prominent, with a well-deserved social status until she meets a white male student that threatens all she holds dear.

Marco Laredo was a cocky soccer player who needed help in history. Passing this one last class would solidify his chances of graduating and entering the Major League

Soccer SuperDraft. Requesting help was easy, but when a fellow student could no longer tutor him, he seeks out Ms. Parcel in desperation.

When the student/teacher collide, fireworks spark. One session turns into a torrid, secret affair.

Read today!

Kindle Unlimited & paperback

Trixi Matthews had always known who her biological father was. Her mother had been a maid in the wealthy businessman's household for years, and Mr. Fischer frequently took advantage of her mother's youth.

Twenty-four years later, Trixi now wants to know him. At first, stalking Mr. Fischer had been easy - she had easily gone unnoticed until she's discovered by the covert operations of his wayward son.

Grayson Fischer had noticed her from the start! Trixi was unlike any girl he'd ever seen - but who was she really?

They meet by chance, and Trixi keeps her secret ... until Grayson begins to show his feelings for her. Find out what happens when the mystery gets revealed.

Part 1 of 2

BWWM Romance

Ebook & Paperback

love child – part 2

Grayson Fischer cannot believe his horrible fate. He's found the woman of his dreams—but she turns out to be his half-sister? What hellish nightmare was this?

Trixi Matthews finally gets to know her biological father, it's all she's ever dreamed of, but her feelings for Grayson make her lovesick with the understanding of the truth.

What happens to Trixi and Grayson? Do they give into their twisted attraction to one another? Or do they go their separate ways, and face eternal heartbreak?

Find out what happens in Part Two of "Love Child - A BWWM Romance"

Part 2 of 2

A BWWM Romance

Ebook & Paperback

Dylan Roxi is an emerging author of BWWM Romance and Contemporary Modern Fiction. Dylan has many writing interests and lives an incognito digital lifestyle.

Dylan is part of the Ardent Artist Books family and is the author of several published books.

amazon.com/Ardent-Artist-Books/e/B08BX8F1DZ

youtube.com/theardentartist

also by dylan

Love Child - Part 1

Love Child - Part 2

Offsides

Almost Yours

Cougar at Play